I CAN MAKE A
TRAIN
NOISE

Books Under the Bridge

CAFÉ

Il Gatto Nero

For Barbara and Ed, with love —M.L.F.
For Roger Emberley —M.E.

Neal Porter Books

Text and illustrations copyright © 2021 by Michael Emberley
and Marie-Louise Fitzpatrick
All Rights Reserved
HOLIDAY HOUSE is registered in the U.S. Patent and Trademark Office.
Printed and bound in March 2021 at C & C Offset, Shenzhen, China.
The artwork for this book was created with acrylic paint, pencil and
digital techniques.
www.holidayhouse.com
First Edition
1 3 5 7 9 10 8 6 4 2

Library of Congress Cataloging-in-Publication Data

Names: Emberley, Michael, author. | Fitzpatrick, Marie-Louise, author.
Title: I can make a train noise / by Michael Emberley and Marie-Louise
Fitzpatrick.
Description: First edition. | New York : Holiday House, [2021] | "A Neal
Porter Book." | Audience: Ages 4 to 6. | Audience: Grades K-1. |
Summary: "A girl transforms a cafe into a train by making train noises
with words"— Provided by publisher.
Identifiers: LCCN 2020025897 | ISBN 9780823444960 (hardcover)
Subjects: CYAC: Railroad trains—Fiction. | Imagination—Fiction.
Classification: LCC PZ7.E566 Iah 2021 | DDC [E]—dc23
LC record available at https://lccn.loc.gov/2020025897   Robots—Fiction.
Classification: LCC PZ8.G286 Li 2021 | DDC [E]—dc23
LC record available at https://lccn.loc.gov/2020025839

ISBN 978-0-8234-4496-0 (hardcover)

Marie-Louise Fitzpatrick received financial assistance
from the Arts Council of Ireland in the form of a literature bursary.

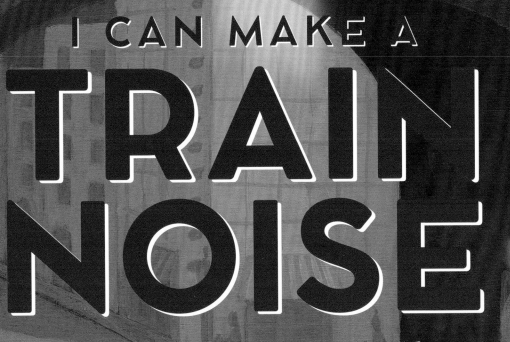

I CAN MAKE A
TRAIN
NOISE

Michael Emberley and
Marie-Louise Fitzpatrick

CAFÉ

Il Gatto Nero

NEAL PORTER BOOKS
HOLIDAY HOUSE / NEW YORK

I can make a train noise, I can make a train

noise, I can make a train noise, **now!**

I can make ^a train noise I can make ^a train noise I can make ^a train no

I can make a train noise I can make a train noise I can make a train no

I can make a train noise,
I can make a train noise,
I can make a train noise, now, now.

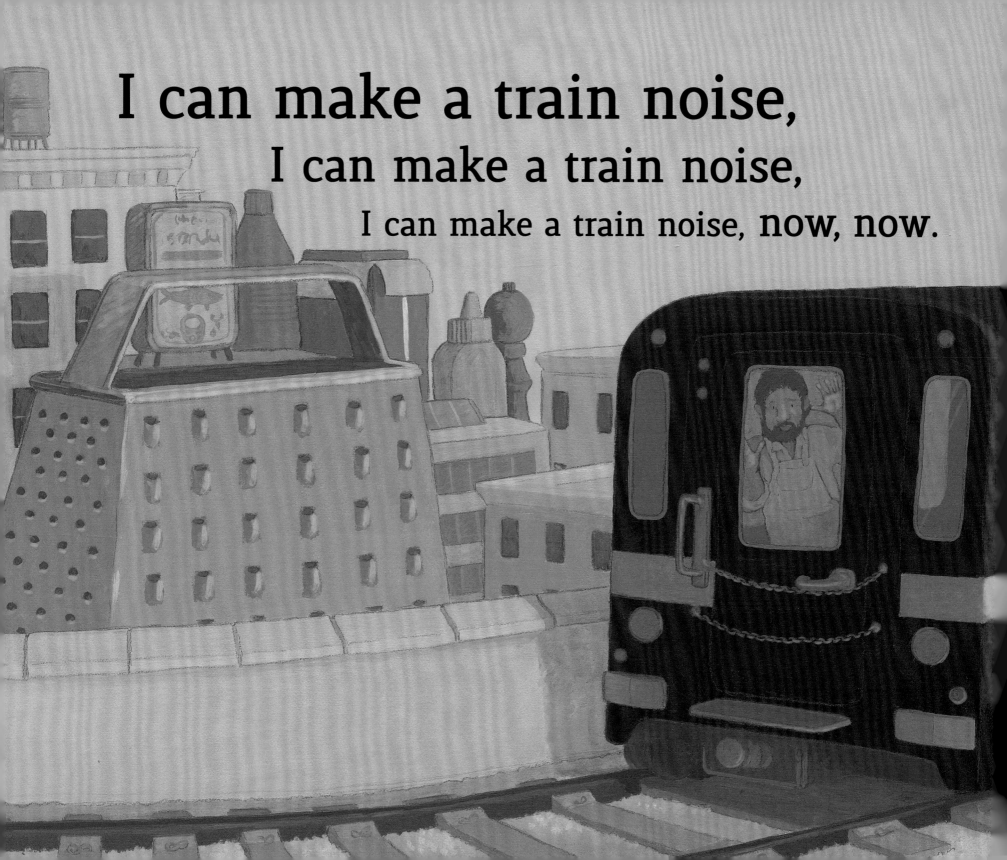

I can make a train noise, I can make a train noise, I can make a train noise . . .

I can make a train noise,

I can make a train noise,

I can make a train noise,

I can make a train noise

I can m

I can make a train noise.

I can make a train noise,

I can make a train noise,

I can make a train noise,

I can make a train noise,

I can make a train noise,

ke a train noise,

I can make a train noise, I can make a train noise, I can make

I can make

train noise, now, now.

rain noise, I can make a train noise, I can make a train noise, now.

I . . . can . . . make . . . a . . . train . . . noise,   I . . . can . . . make . . . a . . . train

I . . . can . . . make . . . a

noise,   I . . . can . . . make . . . a . . . train . . . noise . . . now . . . now . . .

. . train . . . . noise . . . . I . . . . can . . . . make . . . . a . . . . train . . . . noise . . . . .

I . . . . can . . . . make . . . . a . . . . train . . . . nooooiiisssssssssssssse . . .

now!

Can
YOU
make a
train noise?